For Asha and Hannah
and all the mothers and fathers
who only ever get to $2\frac{7}{8}$

First American paperback edition published in 1996 by
Crocodile Books, USA
An imprint of Interlink Publishing Group, Inc.
99 Seventh Avenue, Brooklyn, New York 11215
Text © by Ewa Lipniacka 1991, 1996
Illustrations © by Basia Bogdanowicz 1991, 1996

Published simultaneously in Great Britain by Magi Publications.

Library of Congress Cataloging-in-Publication Data

Lipniacka, Ewa
    To bed -- or else / written by Ewa Lipniacka : illustrated by Basia
Bogdanowicz. -- 1st American ed.
        p.   cm.
    Summary: When Asha spends the night with Hannah, their energetic
refusal to go to bed makes Hannah's mother threaten, "To bed, or else!"
    ISBN 0-940793-85-7(hbk) --- ISBN 1-56656-214-7(pbk)
    [1. Sleepovers -- Fiction. 2. Bedtime -- Fiction.] I. Bogdanowicz, Basia,
ill. II. Title.
PZ7. L6643To 1996
[E] -- dc20
                                                              91-22118
                                                                CIP
                                                                 AC

Printed and bound in Hong Kong
10 9 8 7 6 5 4 3 2 1

To bed · · OR ELSE!

Written by Ewa Lipniacka
Illustrated by Basia Bogdanowicz

Crocodile Books, USA

An imprint of Interlink Publishing Group, Inc.
NEW YORK

HANNAH!

Asha and Hannah lived next door to each other.

They were the best of friends.

They shared their birthdays, their books,
and even some of their toys ...

... most of the time.

Their Moms were also friends, and they shared
too – they shared their children.
If Hannah's Mom had to go out in the evening,
Hannah stayed with Asha.

And if Asha's Mom had to work late,

Asha moved in, with just a few of her things,
to stay at Hannah's.

But the more they were together,
the noisier they would be.
And one night Hannah's Mom just couldn't get them to bed.

She read them a story,

then another,

and another.

She sang bedtime songs,

and made shadows on the wall ...

Still they would not sleep.

Then she got very angry.
"That's it!" she shouted. "By the time
I count to three, you two will be in bed and asleep...
OR ELSE!!!"

"OR ELSE – what?" asked Asha and Hannah, together.
"O-N-E!" yelled Hannah's Mom, heading for the kitchen.
"What happens when she gets to OR ELSE, Hannah?"

"Well, she might shout some more," said Hannah.
"But what if she does something worse?" asked Asha.

"Like put us out for the garbage collector!"

"Or what if she gave all your toys to a rummage sale?"

"T-W-O!" they heard Hannah's Mom call from the kitchen.

"Maybe she would never, ever buy us ice cream again ..."

"... and make us take horrible medicine instead."

"Hannah, she might turn us into frogs!"

"TWO-AND-A-HALF !"

"What if she baked us in a pie like blackbirds,
and served us for dinner?"
"She wouldn't, would she? She couldn't!" wailed Hannah.
"But she might ... " worried Asha.

"Hannah, I'm scared. I don't think I want to find out
what OR ELSE means."
"Me neither," said Hannah.
"Let's go to sleep – fast."
"Yes, let's."

And believe it or not – they did.

"Thank goodness," thought Hannah's Mom, as
she cleared up the mess and tucked them in.

"I just don't know what I would have done
if they hadn't gone to sleep!"